Zoolidays

Written by Bruce Glassman · Illustrated by Rolandas Kiaulevicius

red
cygnet™
PRESS

San Diego, California

red
cygnet™
P R E S S

In memory of Gini Mariotti.
Special thanks to Jack, Karen, Michael, Kay, Robert, Vladimir, Abe and Leslie. – R.K.

Illustrations copyright © 2007 Rolandas Kiaulevicius
Manuscript copyright © 2007 Bruce Glassman
Book copyright © 2007 Red Cygnet Press, Inc., 11858 Stoney Peak Dr. #525, San Diego, CA 92128

Cover and book design: Amy Stirnkorb

First Edition 2007
10 9 8 7 6 5 4 3 2
Printed in China

Library of Congress Cataloging-in-Publication Data
is available at our website: www.redcygnet.com

At nine in the morning
at the Metro Park Zoo
the gates are unlocked
so the kids can walk
through.

Hand in hand
with a mom,
a teacher, or dad,
the kids all expect
the best time
ever had.

One day was quite
different,
not the usual day,
the kids were not
smiling
their usual way.

No giggles, no laughter,
no jumps up and down,
just stony, cold faces
all frozen in frown.

The animals saw this,
some even protested,
"how can these kids
be so uninterested?"

The tigers got touchy,
they raged and they
roared,
they showed off
their claws,
but the kids just
looked bored.

The deer started sobbing
when their beautiful fawns
had little effect
but to stir up some yawns.

Seeing this trouble,
the pigeons took wing
and told all the animals
of this terrible thing.

They flew to the pandas,
they flew to the yaks,
they flew to the hippos,
and told them the facts.

"The kids have lost interest"
they squawked loud and clear,
"we have to do something
to keep them all here!"

By twelve o'clock noon
the patrons had gone,
no one was left
not a kid, not a mom.

The animals panicked,
they fretted and paced,
"what a terrible day,"
"what a terrible waste".

The zoo's chief director
upon hearing the news
said closing the zoo's the
only thing she could choose.

The pigeons all heard this
and took to their flight,
they relayed the message
well into the night.

"What can we do?"
the walruses whined,
"we're in quite a pickle,
we're in quite a bind."

"We have an idea,"
the peacocks proclaimed,
"let's jazz ourselves up,
and all be re-named."

"Forget what you used to be,
forget what you were,
instead let's paint patterns
on our skins and our fur."

"We'll be totally famous
when everyone hears
and our zoo will stay open
for ten thousand years!"

"The place will be awesome,
the children will say,
they'll start calling their visits
a real Zooliday!"

The animals cheered,
then went to their stations
to begin working on
their greatest creations...

The panthers painted
mother moose
in a forest made of blue,
and moose adorned
the guinea hens
as they lined up
two by two.

Baby roo and
mommy kanga
put koalas into stripes
when their brown
paint had dried a bit
into spots of
many types.

Frog and fly felt
fairly sure
their work would
not be beaten—
fly, for sure,
felt quite a buzz
cuzz he had not
been eaten.

Spattered speckles hit the emu
as lizard flecked and flicked,
he much enjoyed his racing stripes
and the colors that he'd picked.

The bear cub took his little brush
and crawled to elephant's knees,
they both began to illustrate
a swarm of honey bees.

A sea of squid the
monkey made
upon the giant sow,
he came covered red
with curlicues
(though no one
quite knew how).

Hippo had parrots
on his back
to paint their
paisley art,
he helped to hold
the blue paint pail
when their easels
fell apart.

A bright green swamp on crocodile
meant leaves from tail to snout,
some birds striped his mouth inside
as they darted in and out.

The bats were happy hanging 'round
acting kind of tough,
but hanging upside down they found
their painting dripped right off!

Chameleon and
orangutan
both joined the
painting fun,
chameleon painted
swirly swirls
with blue ink on
his tongue.

They worked and worked, and worked some more
'til midnight finally came,
under the moon each gathered 'round
to announce his new-found name.

"I'm a paisley-pot-a-miss,"
"and I'm a swamp-o-dile,"
"and I'm a busy buzz-a-phant,
with class, panache, and style"

"We're Art-imals,"
the donkeys brayed,
which scared the snowshoe hare,
"we are unique to all the world,
nothing like us anywhere!"

When morning came, the line outside
was short and somewhat thin,
the kids and dads and moms were not
excited to get in.

A voice from way inside the park
yelled "hey, come look at this!"
the others ran to see the thing,
the "paisley pot-a-miss."

Someone yelled from another place
"hey, come and look inside!"
"a curlicued orangutan
and a sow's blue squiddy hide!"

When a young
girl saw the
South Pole tank
she saw the
walrus wink,
she squealed a squeal
in pure delight,
adoring all
his ink.

The news got out and
traveled fast,
they were mobbed by
a quarter-to,
kids of every shape
and size
swarmed into the zoo.

"It's nothing short
of a miracle,"
the director had exclaimed,
"something that is
never seen,
and cannot be
well explained."

Soon everyday the lines were long (the animals loved this sight), Zoolidays were such a hit they were open every night.

The animals changed
their dots and stripes
just every now
and then,
but the patrons smiled
no matter what
and never
yawned again.